The Eagle
&
the Wren

A fable retold by
Jane Goodall
Illustrated by
Alexander Reichstein

A Michael Neugebauer Book
North-South Books / New York / London

*O*NCE upon a time, long, long ago,
the birds got into an argument about who
could fly the highest.

"I can fly so high," said the skylark, "that I become just a tiny speck in the sky and then I disappear altogether. You can only hear my voice, my beautiful song. I can fly the highest."

"No, no, no," said the dove. "I can fly the highest. I was sent by Noah to search for signs of the ending of the great flood. From high in the sky I flew to pick the olive branch that has become a symbol of peace. I can fly the highest."

"I can fly even higher," said the vulture.
I circle up and up and up until I can look across
half the world. That's how I see my dinner –
the animals who have died. I can fly the highest."

"You are all wrong," said the majestic eagle. "I am the king of the birds. My wings are strong. My heart is great. I fly far above the world and look down to see all that is going on below. I can fly the highest."

"Be silent, all of you," said the wise owl.
"We will have a contest for all the birds.
We will find out just how high each
one of us can fly."

So all the birds took to the air.
There was a great flapping of wings, and squawking
and calling and hooting and croaking.

Some of the birds didn't fly
very high at all. They quickly
came back to earth. They were
a bit sad, but the ostrich welcomed
them.

"You have all done as well as nature
intended," he said.

"You all have wings, but each of you
flies to a different height for a different
purpose. After all," he added,

"I can't fly and I'm certainly not ashamed
of that. I use my wings in the beautiful
dance that wins me my bride."

Some of the birds flew very high indeed.

But after a while many of them
grew tired and could fly no higher.
So they came back to earth.
The vulture saw a dead animal
and was suddenly so hungry,
he dived down and out of the contest.

Just a few birds were able to keep on flying.

*Eventually the skylark and
the dove came down too.
They couldn't go any higher.*

In the end they could see only one
bird still up in the sky – so high,
he seemed to be almost in heaven.

It was the eagle.

Finally even he could fly no higher. Tired
but proud, he hovered way, way up in the sky.
"I knew I would win," he said to himself.

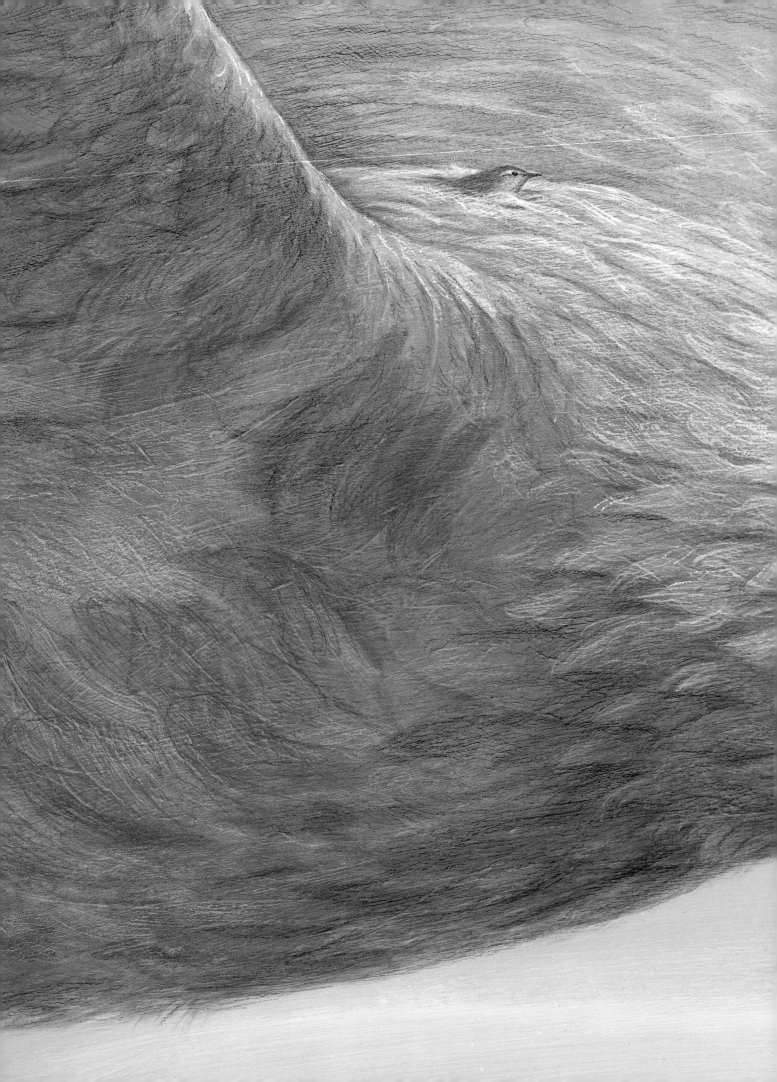

But as the mighty eagle soared high above the earth, something crept out from among his thick feathers.

To the eagle's amazement, he saw a tiny bird –
the little wren – flying even higher than he was.
He tried and tried to get above her,
but he was too tired.

"How did you fly so high?" he asked her.

She laughed — a tiny laugh because she was such a tiny bird.

"You carried me all the way," she said.

"I couldn't have flown so high by myself.

But don't worry, you won `the contest."

"I always wondered what the world looked like from high, high up
at the top of the sky. Now I know.
I shall always remember this. Thank you."

When they got back to earth, they told their story to the
other birds. The owl praised them both.
"Together you have set a new record," he told them.
"With your strong wings and determination, mighty
Eagle, and with your dreaming and your quick brain,
little Wren, you have flown to a height never reached
by any bird before."

First published in Switzerland under the title **Der Adler und der Zaunkönig**
Text copyright © 2000 by Jane Goodall
Illustrations copyright © 2000 by Michael Neugebauer Verlag,
an imprint of Nord-Süd Verlag AG, Gossau Zürich, Switzerland

First published in the United States, Great Britain, Canada,
Australia, and New Zealand in 2000 by North-South Books,
an imprint of Nord-Süd Verlag AG, Gossau Zürich, Switzerland.

Distributed in the United States by North-South Books Inc., New York.

Library of Congress Cataloging-in-Publication Data is available.
A CIP catalogue record for this book is available from The British Library.
ISBN 0-7358-1380-9 (trade binding) 10 9 8 7 6 5 4 3 2 1
ISBN 0-7358-1381-7 (library binding) 10 9 8 7 6 5 4 3 2 1
Printed in Belgium

Ask your bookseller for the other children's books written by Jane Goodall:
THE CHIMPANZEE FAMILY BOOK, photos by Michael Neugebauer
WITH LOVE, illustrated by Alan Marks
DR WHITE, illustrated by Julie Litty

For more information about our books, and the authors and artists
who create them, visit our web site: www.northsouth.com

When we were small, my sister, Judy, and I had a story read to us every night. This is one of those stories, and I still love it.

It is like an illustration of our life on Earth. None of us can fly very high by ourselves. We all need an eagle. We need the help of other people as we struggle upward. I have been very fortunate in my life. I have been helped by many, many people: wonderful friends; the students who help collect the information about chimpanzees; the supporters who help to carry out our various projects and those who help us to raise the money for them; my terrific family – my grandmother, my aunts, and my sister; and, most specially, my mother, who has been there to help and guide me all through my life.

I like to think of all these people as the feathers on my eagle. Each one has played an important role. Some of them are like big strong feathers. I think my mother is the center tail feather, helping to steer me in the right direction. Some people are the strong wing feathers, beating the air. Others are the soft downy feathers that nestle round you when you are tired and old. Each one is valued.

And what about the eagle? I suppose we all have different eagles. But I know that my eagle is part of the great spirit power that is all around us, from which we can draw strength and energy when most we need it. I thank my eagle for carrying me so high.

JANE GOODALL